Dear Parents:

Congratulations! Your child is taking the first steps on an exciting journey. The destination? Independent reading!

STEP INTO READING® will help your child get there. The program offers five steps to reading success. Each step includes fun stories and colorful art or photographs. In addition to original fiction and books with favorite characters, there are Step into Reading Non-Fiction Readers, Phonics Readers and Boxed Sets, Sticker Readers, and Comic Readers—a complete literacy program with something to interest every child.

Learning to Read, Step by Step!

Ready to Read **Preschool–Kindergarten**
• big type and easy words • rhyme and rhythm • picture clues
For children who know the alphabet and are eager to begin reading.

Reading with Help **Preschool–Grade 1**
• basic vocabulary • short sentences • simple stories
For children who recognize familiar words and sound out new words with help.

Reading on Your Own **Grades 1–3**
• engaging characters • easy-to-follow plots • popular topics
For children who are ready to read on their own.

Reading Paragraphs **Grades 2–3**
• challenging vocabulary • short paragraphs • exciting stories
For newly independent readers who read simple sentences with confidence.

Ready for Chapters **Grades 2–4**
• chapters • longer paragraphs • full-color art
For children who want to take the plunge into chapter books but still like colorful pictures.

STEP INTO READING® is designed to give every child a successful reading experience. The grade levels are only guides; children will progress through the steps at their own speed, developing confidence in their reading.

Remember, a lifetime love of reading starts with a single step!

To all the little girls lifting their voice
to make a difference —B.A.

 Published in the United States by Random House Children's Books, a division of Penguin Random House LLC, 1745 Broadway, New York, NY 10019, and in Canada by Penguin Random House Canada Limited, Toronto.

Step into Reading, Random House, and the Random House colophon are registered trademarks of Penguin Random House LLC.

Visit us on the web!
StepIntoReading.com
rhcbooks.com

Educators and librarians, for a variety of teaching tools, visit us at RHTeachersLibrarians.com

ISBN 978-0-593-43169-6 (trade) — ISBN 978-0-593-43170-2 (lib. bdg.)
ISBN 978-0-593-43171-9 (ebook)

Printed in the United States of America
10 9 8 7 6 5 4 3 2 1

Random House Children's Books supports the First Amendment and celebrates the right to read.

STEP 3 READING ON YOUR OWN

American Girl®

Melody
Lifts Her Voice

by Bria Alston
illustrated by Parker-Nia Gordon
and Shiane Salabie
Based on a story by Denise Lewis Patrick

Random House New York

Meet Melody Ellison!

Melody is a ten-year-old girl

who lives in Detroit in 1964.

She loves to sing and garden.

She has two sisters,

a brother who is a musician,

and a dog named Bo.

On New Year's Eve, Melody attends
Watch Night service at church
with her parents, sisters,
and grandparents,
Big Momma and Poppa.

Melody and her friends
and family call church
their "home away from home."

Before the service begins,

Melody's cousin Val whispers,

"It's almost your birthday!"

Melody grins as the service starts.

"Good evening, friends!"

Pastor Daniels says.

“Good evening!” everyone calls back.
Pastor Daniels invites everybody
to pick one thing they want
to change for the better
in the coming year,
right here in their community.

After the service, families eat cake and drink punch in the church hall. Melody's big sister Yvonne shares her idea to make change.

She will teach kids
about Black history and civil rights
over the summer. Melody thinks
about Pastor Daniels's message.
How can *she* make
a difference?

The next day is Melody's birthday!

At her party, everyone cheers,

"Happy birthday, Melody!"

Melody misses her brother, Dwayne.

He is away, touring with his band.

"Happy birthday to you,
my kid sister, Dee-Dee!"
sings a voice at the door.
"Dwayne!" Melody shouts.
She is surprised and so happy!

A week later, the adults in Melody's
neighborhood gather for a meeting.
The kids hear them talk about
how unfairly Fieldston's clothing store
has treated Black people.
Melody knows this is true. . . .

She speaks up. “When I went
shopping at Fieldston’s with Dwayne,
the manager accused us of stealing,
just because we’re Black.”

“That’s wrong!” her father says.

The grown-ups decide to boycott the store.

Boycotting means not shopping
at the store. It's a way to protest
how the store treats people.
Melody talks to Val and her friends.
They want to boycott the store, too.

Everyone gathers to march.

They lift their voices in protest.

They sing and hold signs.

Melody is proud to speak up

for her rights.

Still, Melody wishes she could make her own change. The next day, she takes her dog, Bo, for a walk to the playground.

It used to be a fun place.

Now there is litter everywhere.
Melody wonders what she can do.
She has an idea to plant a garden
and clean up the playground.
"This is what I can change!"
Melody says.

Melody tells her friends about
her plan to fix up the playground
and plant a garden. They form a club
and elect Melody president.
They want to make the park
a fun space for the community.

Melody tells her family her plans.

Everyone loves her ideas!

She hopes the park will be ready

in time for the neighborhood's

annual summer picnic.

The work at the playground begins!
Melody and her friends
work hard, but they don't
know how to do everything.
And they are a small group.
Melody worries that she
is not a good president.

Poppa stops by to help.

He encourages Melody.

"A leader doesn't have to do everything herself," he says.

Melody asks her friends to bring tools and more kids to help with the work.

Dwayne asks Melody for help, too. He wants her to sing on his record! Dwayne plays the piano as Melody practices the song. The next day, she sings the song in a real music studio.

At the playground, more kids come to help. Melody hums Dwayne's song. It's catchy! Soon the other kids are humming it, too.

The week of the picnic,
A big storm hits.
Their hard work is ruined!
Melody is discouraged.

"We were all done,"
she says sadly.
"A garden is never finished,"
Poppa replies. "Gardens
and good works keep going,
but both need tending."

Back home, Melody calls her friends.

They meet in the park,

ready to keep going.

More kids arrive to lend a hand.

With some sunshine
and everyone working together,
the gardens bounce back
and the park gets restored.

On the day of the summer picnic,
the park is as good as new!
Neighbors thank Melody
and her friends
for fixing up the park.

Melody thanks her family and friends for their support. With their help, she was able to change her community as Pastor Daniels suggested.

Melody and Dwayne perform their song. Her heart is full. She knows she has made a difference.

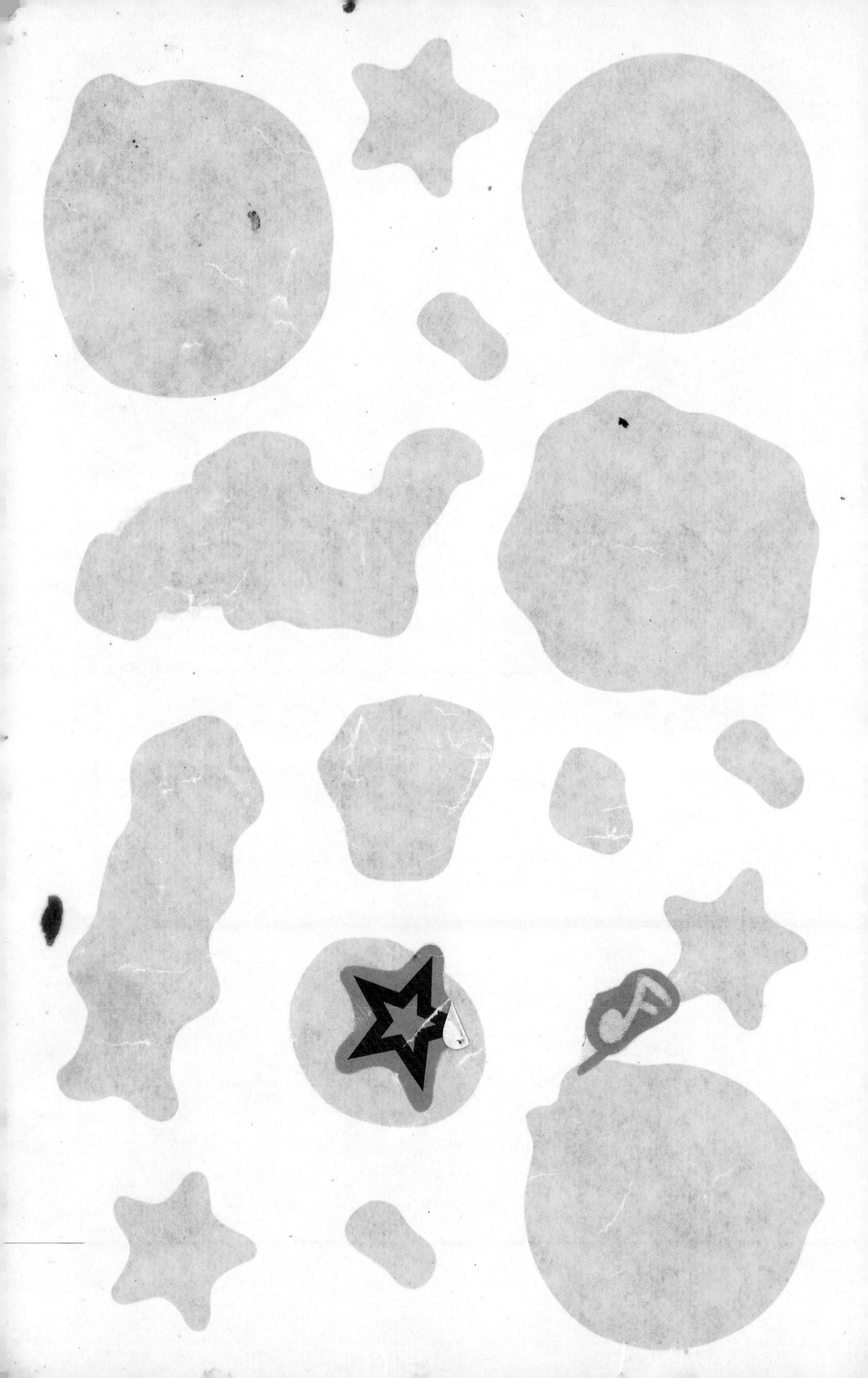